Creations

Presents

Fast, Far and Free

A Tale of Three Special Friends

Fast, Far and Free
A Tale of Three Special Friends

by **Audra Doyle**

Illustrated by
Daniel and **Audra Doyle**

Two Harbors Press
Minneapolis, MN

Two Harbors Press
322 First Avenue N, 5th floor
Minneapolis, MN 55401
612.455.2293
www.TwoHarborsPress.com

ISBN-13: 978-1-62652-752-2
LCCN: 2014903682

Distributed by Itasca Books

Book Design by Sophie Chi

Printed in the United States of America

Dedicated to our babies

Interactive questions can be found throughout the book in talking bubbles just like this one!

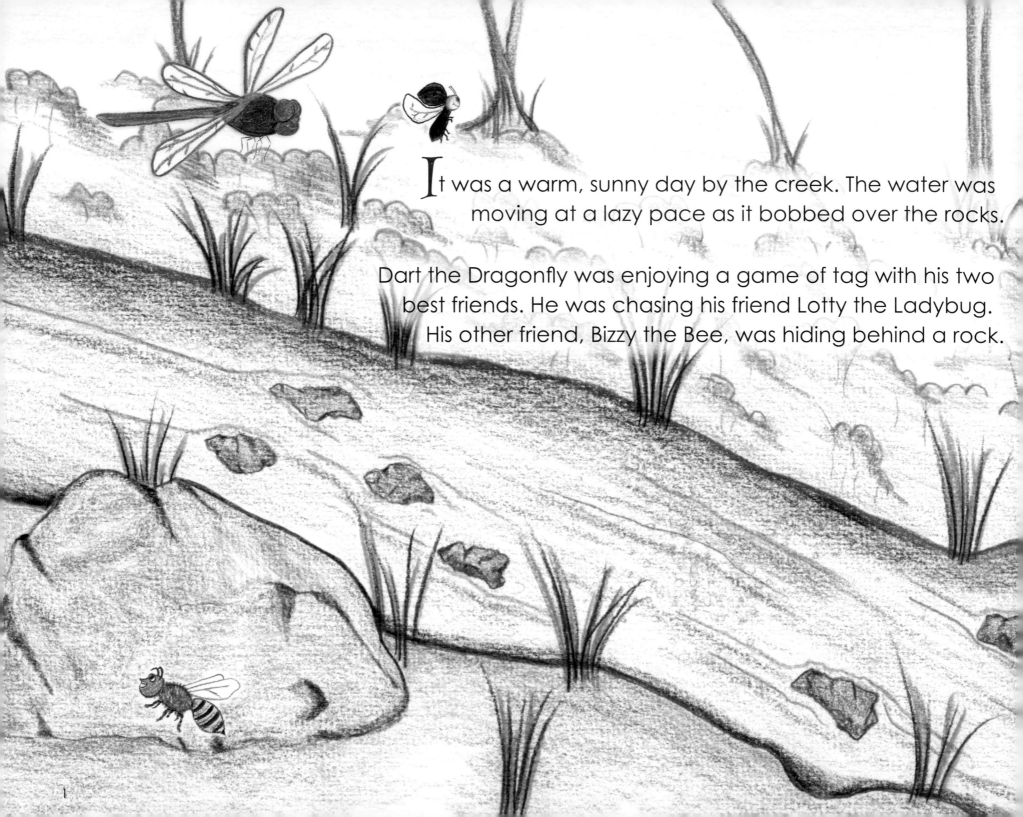

It was a warm, sunny day by the creek. The water was moving at a lazy pace as it bobbed over the rocks.

Dart the Dragonfly was enjoying a game of tag with his two best friends. He was chasing his friend Lotty the Ladybug. His other friend, Bizzy the Bee, was hiding behind a rock.

"I caught you again, Lotty Dotty!" Dart exclaimed.
He liked to call her that because she had lots of dots.

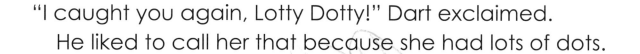

"No fair," pouted Lotty. "You're too fast!"
"Hey, you know me, I fly fast, far and free,"
Dart laughed.

Do you have a nickname?
If you could choose your nickname,
what would it be?

2

Dart was the fastest of all his friends and he proudly let them know it.
His friends had special abilities too. He just never slowed down to notice.

"Lotty Dotty's it!" he told his friend Bizzy.
"She'll never catch me," said Bizzy. "I'm superfast!"

"I'm faster than you," Dart bragged, "and I can prove it. Let's race."
"Okay," Bizzy said. He knew his friend was fast but he still wanted to try.
"I thought we were playing tag. Why do you have to race?" asked Lotty.
"It will be fun," Dart replied. "Do you want to race too, Lotty Dotty?"

What makes Dart special?

4

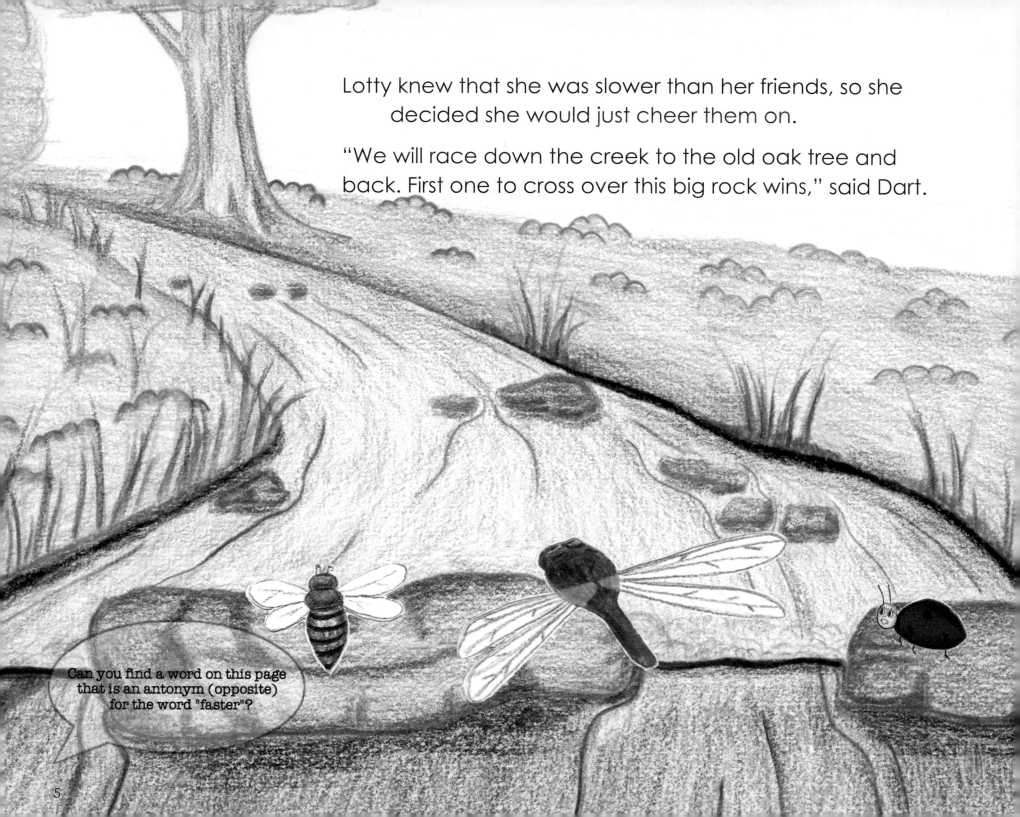

Lotty knew that she was slower than her friends, so she decided she would just cheer them on.

"We will race down the creek to the old oak tree and back. First one to cross over this big rock wins," said Dart.

Can you find a word on this page that is an antonym (opposite) for the word "faster"?

"I'm ready," Bizzy said excitedly, but he was also feeling nervous. "Tell us when to go, Lotty."

Lotty called out, "On your mark . . . , get set . . . , GO!"

And they were off! Bizzy the Bee was fast,
but Dart the Dragonfly was faster.
He quickly took the lead.

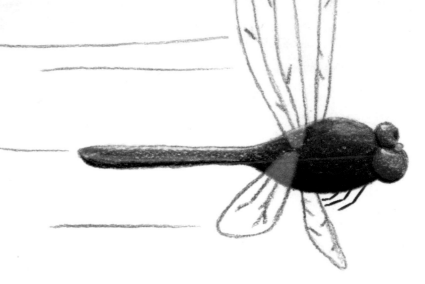

Bizzy didn't give up.
He was determined to do his best even if he didn't win.

What makes Bizzy special?

They were flying so swiftly that they didn't notice when they passed over a very big and hungry fish.

Lotty saw the big fish move and knew her friends were in danger.

When they reached the old oak tree,
they zipped around to race towards the finish line.

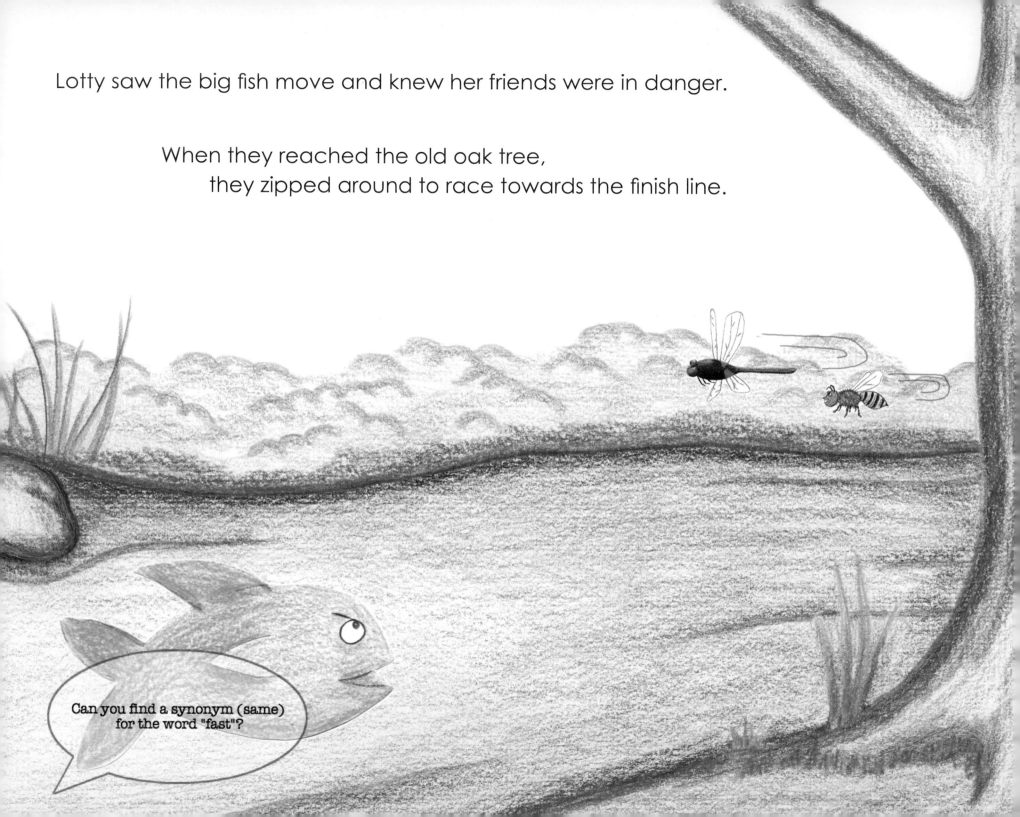

Can you find a synonym (same) for the word "fast"?

The fish saw them turning around.

He was waiting for them to pass by
so he could jump out of the water and gulp them up with his big mouth.

Lotty had no way to warn her friends.
She had to think fast.

Lotty flew toward the big fish
and flapped her wings rapidly to try to distract him.

Her plan worked.

He stopped waiting for Dart and Bizzy
and went after her!

Can you find another synonym
for the word "fast"?

12

Lotty was scared but she was also very brave.
She quickly used her legs to make a stinky and bad-tasting oil.

Then the big fish jumped out of the water
and swallowed her up!

But Lotty was ready for this to happen. As soon as the fish tasted the bad oil she had made, he spit her out and said, "Yuck! Yuck!"

He swam away. He certainly wasn't hungry anymore. Lotty was free and her friends were safe.

Dart and Bizzy saw what happened.
They hurried to her side.
"Lotty Dotty, are you okay?" asked Dart.

"Yes," said Lotty, feeling tired and weak.
"That big fish was going to gobble you up.
I couldn't let that happen!"

What makes Lotty special?

Dart always thought he was extra special because he could fly fast, far and free.

Lotty showed him that she had a special gift too.
She knew how to defend herself by making a yucky oil with her legs.

Dart realized that Lotty put herself in danger to save his life, and Bizzy's too.
She did something only a brave ladybug could do.
She was special. She was a hero!
She was a really good friend.

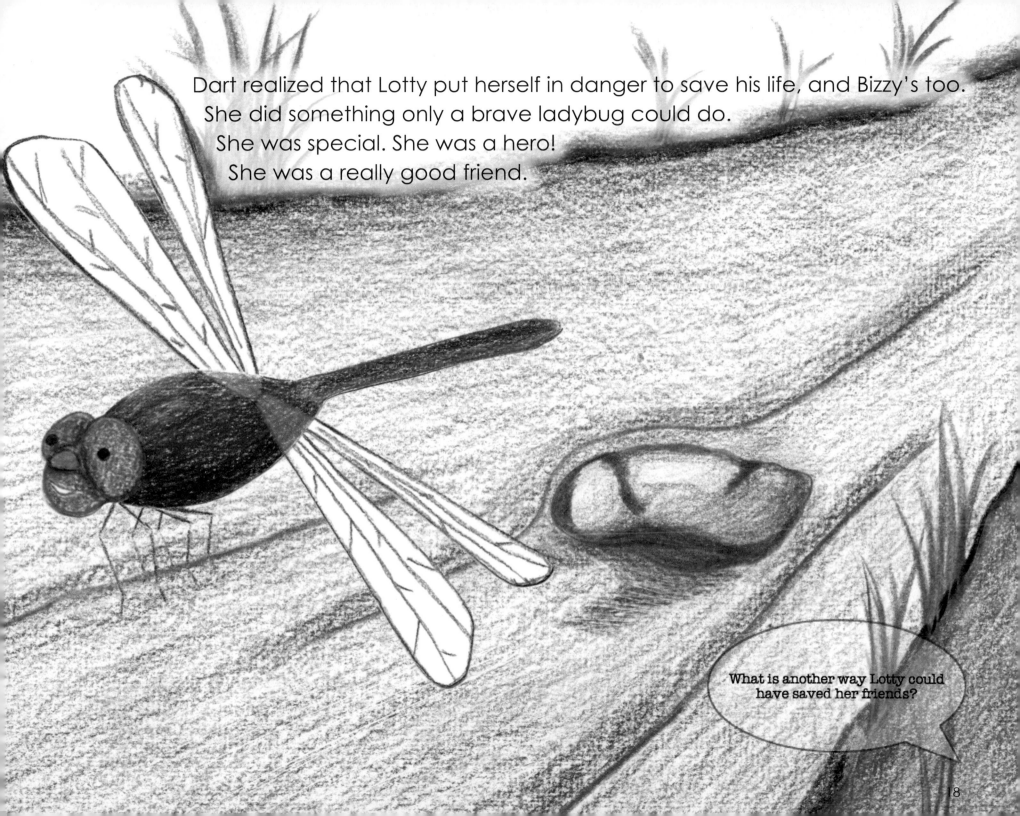

What is another way Lotty could have saved her friends?

18

"Thank you, Lotty," said Dart and Bizzy.
Feeling weary but happy, Lotty joked,
"Hey, you know me, I fly slow, smart and free."
They all laughed.

They were thankful for their friends.

What makes YOU special?

19

The End

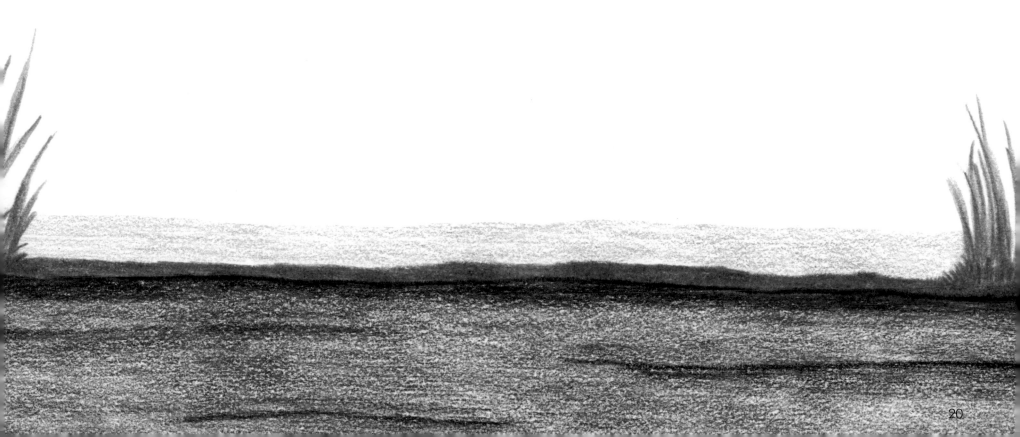

True True or Cuckoo?

Can you tell which statements are really true and which ones are really silly (cuckoo)?

1. Ladybugs can make oil with their legs.
2. Dragonflies are the fastest flying insects.
3. Bees and dragonflies are friends.
4. Fish eat dragonflies.
5. Dragonflies can talk.
6. Dragonflies can fly far.
7. Fish eat bees.
8. Dragonflies and ladybugs are friends.
9. Fish eat ladybugs.
10. Bees fly faster than ladybugs.

Answer Key

1. True True: Ladybugs produce bad-tasting and bad-smelling yellow oil that they make to defend themselves from their predators.
2. True True: The Australian dragonfly flies at a steady speed of 25 miles per hour and can reach speeds of 35 miles per hour when traveling shorter distances.
3. Cuckoo
4. True True: Fish prefer smaller insects but will eat dragonflies if they must.
5. Cuckoo
6. True True: Scientists believe the Globe Skimmer dragonfly makes a yearly trip from India to East Africa—a round-trip of 11,000 miles!
7. Cuckoo
8. Cuckoo
9. Cuckoo
10. True True: A honeybee flies about 15 miles per hour and a ladybug flies about 5 miles per hour.

Please visit
www.fastfarandfree.com
for more fun facts
and interactive games!